Friends

Friends

written and illustrated by
Helme Heine

Aladdin Books
Macmillan Publishing Company   *New York*

Every morning, when Charlie Rooster strutted into the barn to wake the other animals, Johnny Mouse and fat Percy went with him to help. "Good friends always stick together," they said. When this job was done, they wheeled their bicycle out of the barn and set off for their morning ride.

They could ride down the roughest paths and up the steepest cliffs.

No curve was too sharp for them and their bicycle.
No puddle was deep enough to stop them.

One day, they played a game of hide-and-seek
by the village pond.

While Johnny Mouse was hiding, he discovered an old boat lying in the tall grass. He showed his friends, and they decided to play pirates. "Good friends always decide things together," they said.

Johnny Mouse took the tiller, Charlie Rooster opened his wings to make the sail, and fat Percy plugged up the hole in the side of the boat by sitting on it.

They sailed out on the open water, and as the day
went on, they felt very brave and bold. They
conquered the village pond!

But hunger finally sent them back to the shore.

First they tried to catch a fish. But their stomachs rumbled so loudly that they frightened all the fish away.

Then they went looking for cherries. They shared them: some for Johnny Mouse, some for Charlie Rooster, and twice as many for fat Percy.

Johnny Mouse didn't mind, but Charlie Rooster complained. He said it was unfair. So they gave him the cherry stones. "Friends are always fair," they said.

They ate so many cherries that they all got stomachaches and had to sit down for a while before they started back.

As evening fell and the shadows grew longer

they bicycled home.

Behind the henhouse, near the water barrel, they swore to be friends forever.

"Good friends always stick together," they said.

They decided to spend the night in Johnny Mouse's house. But Charlie Rooster got stuck in the doorway.

Then fat Percy invited them to spend the night with him; but Johnny Mouse said he didn't want to sleep in a pigsty.

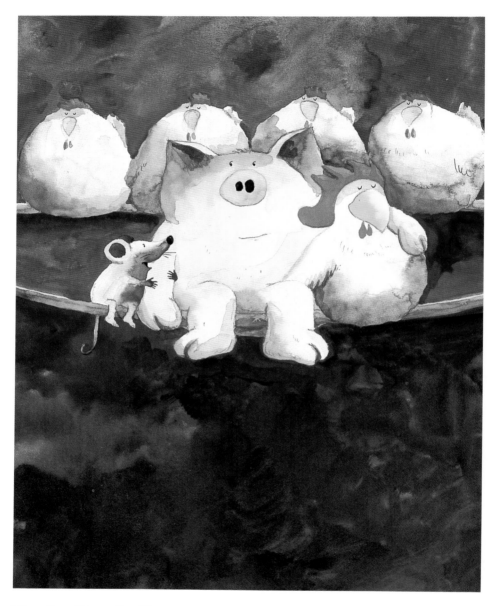

Finally, Charlie Rooster suggested sleeping in the henhouse. They tried to rest on a perch high above the ground...

but it broke. So, sadly, they said good night to each other and went to their own beds. "Sometimes good friends can't be together," they said.

But that night they dreamed about each other, the way true friends do.

Aladdin Books, Macmillan Publishing Company, 866 Third Avenue, New York, NY 10022. Collier Macmillan Canada, Inc.
First Aladdin Books edition 1986. Printed in the United States of America. A hardcover edition of *Friends* is available from
Margaret K. McElderry Books, Macmillan Publishing Company.
11   13   15   17   19   20   18   16   14   12
Published originally under the title: *Freunde* by Helme Heine by Gertraud Middelhauve Verlag, Köln.
Library of Congress Cataloging-in-Publication Data: Heine, Helme. Friends. Translation of: Freunde. Summary: Three friends w
love to be together come to the realization that sometimes it's just not possible. [1. Animals—Fiction. 2. Friendship—Fiction]
I. Title. PZ7.H3678Fr   1986   [E]   86-3379   ISBN 0-689-71083-6 (pbk.)